CONTENTS

CHAPTER 1

A return 7

CHAPTER 2

Teach a teacher . . . 14

CHAPTER 3

It's not easy! 21

CHAPTER 4

Cartwheels 30

GRACIE *and The*

NAME: Gracie LaRoo

TEAM: Water Sprites

CLAIM TO FAME:
Being the youngest pig
to join a world-renowned
synchronized swimming team!

SIGNATURE MOVE:
"When Pigs Fly" Spin

LIKES: Purple, clip-on tail bows,
mud baths, new-mown hay
smell

DISLIKES: Too much attention,
doing laundry, scary films

QUOTE

"I just hope I can be the kind of synchronized
swimmer my team needs!"

GRACIE La Roo
GOES TO SCHOOL

written by **MARSHA QUALEY**
illustrated by **KRISTYNA LITTEN**

raintree 🦋

Raintree is an imprint of Capstone Global Library
Limited, a company incorporated in England and
Wales having its registered office at 264 Banbury
Road, Oxford, OX2 7DY – Registered company
number: 6695582

www.raintree.co.uk
myorders@raintree.co.uk

Text © Capstone Global Library Limited 2018
The moral rights of the proprietor have been asserted.

Edited by Megan Atwood
Designed by Aruna Rangarajan
Illustrated by Kristyna Litten
Production by Steve Walker
Printed and bound in China

ISBN 978 1 474 74473 7
21 20 19 18 17
10 9 8 7 6 5 4 3 2 1

British Library Cataloguing in Publication Data
A full catalogue record for this book is available from
the British Library.

WATER SPRITES

JINI

BARB

JIA

SU

MARTHA

BRADY

SILVIA

CHAPTER 1

A RETURN

As soon as Gracie LaRoo stepped out of the taxi, the front door of the school opened and a passel of piglets ran out.

They shouted and ran towards Gracie, surrounding her. She was so excited – and nervous – to be back at her old school.

A student in black-rimmed glasses said, "I'm Ham Edwards. I interviewed you on the phone last winter for our school newspaper, *The Squeal.*"

"I remember!" Gracie said. "That was fun answering your questions."

"I think your speech will be great!" said Ham.

Suddenly Gracie wanted to disappear, but she knew she couldn't. She had to give a speech to the school about being a synchronized swimmer with her team, the Water Sprites.

Gracie could hold her breath underwater for a long time. She could roll across a row of her teammates' hooves and not get dizzy. She could even be lifted into the air and not giggle when her teammates held her hocks – her most ticklish spot.

But she had never given a speech. She wasn't sure she could do it.

"You're going to show us how you swim, right?" a piglet asked her.

Gracie nodded. "Yes, I get to teach a class for you before the speech! I think we will have fun."

She loved teaching piglets
to swim. That was why she had
agreed to visit her old school in
the first place.

The piglets cheered and began
pushing her towards the front
door of the school.

"We are supposed to take you to the headmistress," one said.

"Oh, no!" Gracie said, pretending to be worried. "Am I in trouble?"

The piglets giggled and everyone went inside.

CHAPTER 2

TEACH A TEACHER

Clop, clop, clop.

Fast steps came down the hall.

Gracie spun around.

A tall sow marched towards

Gracie and the piglets.

Gracie hugged her bag.

Butterflies filled her tummy.

Don't be scared, she thought.

You're not a piglet in school

anymore.

Gracie said, "Hello,

Headmistress Pekoni."

The headmistress didn't reply.

She clapped her hooves and said,

"Good job, pupils. Now back to

your classrooms. Shoo, shoo!"

The piglets scattered.

Headmistress Pekoni said, "Welcome back, Gracie LaRoo." She wrinkled her snout. "You used to visit my office a lot when you went to school here. If I remember correctly."

Gracie remembered the last time she was sent to Headmistress Pekoni's office. The week before she left school she had got into trouble for doing cartwheels in the library.

The headmistress said, "We

changed the plan for your class.

There are too many piglets to fit

in the pool, and we didn't think it

was fair to pick just a few. But we

have a volunteer for you. One of

the teachers."

Oh, no! Gracie thought. *How can I teach a teacher?*

Headmistress Pekoni said, "After that you will give your speech. Are you ready?"

Gracie said, "I wrote one . . . But now I think it might be more fun for the students if they could just ask me questions. Like Ham Edwards did for the school paper."

Headmistress Pekoni's eyes opened wide. "It's not supposed to be fun. You are here to lecture the students about the hard work of being a champion athlete. Now follow me, and I will show you where to change for your class."

Gracie felt very small and very young. She looked at the headmistress and said, "Yes, Miss."

IT'S NOT EASY!

The piglets were crowded on the benches by a pool behind the school. They cheered when Gracie walked out in her red and white swimming costume.

She looked around for the teacher who had volunteered.

Only one other pig wore a swimming costume – Coach.

I can't teach him! Gracie

thought. *He scared me when I went*

to school here.

Headmistress Pekoni hushed

the students. She lectured to

them about exercise and physical

fitness.

While she talked, Coach

joined Gracie.

"It's a lot of fuss for your visit," he said.

Gracie's legs felt like melted cheese. Why had she ever agreed to visit the school?

Coach leaned closer. "If you ask me, this is a big hullabaloo for something that isn't even a sport."

Not a sport! Before Gracie could reply, though, Headmistress Pekoni called her name.

Gracie heard Coach chuckle as she walked towards the pool. *Don't let him scare you,* she told herself. *Just be yourself and swim!*

First, Gracie demonstrated moves.

The Dolphin Arch.

The Crane.

The Tub.

After that performance, Gracie

felt like a champion again.

"You can never touch the bottom, even with jumps," she said to the pupils. "That is against the rules in my sport."

She pointed at Coach. "It's your turn to try."

Coach acted scared and all the piglets laughed.

So he doesn't think this is a sport, huh?, Gracie thought.

Gracie showed Coach what to do so he would not touch the bottom of the pool.

"This is called sculling," she said. "Make fast circles with your hooves."

Coach tried his best, but he had to grab the side of the pool.

Gracie demonstrated what a ballet leg looks like.

Coach only rolled over.

"Let's give him something easy," Gracie said to the pupils. "How long can Coach hold his breath?"

Coach sank underwater.

Gracie counted with the audience.

Before they got to 20, Coach

burst into the air. "I was wrong!"

he shouted. "This is very hard!"

CHAPTER 4

CARTWHEELS

The lecture theatre was packed. It was time for her speech.

Gracie twisted the papers in her hooves, crumpling the words she had written earlier.

"Are you okay, kid?" Coach asked.

Gracie said, "I don't feel very well. I have never given a speech."

Coach patted her on the shoulder. "You'll be great. It's time for me to introduce you."

He walked up to the microphone and said, "Let me tell you about our visitor. She is a champion athlete. Today she showed me a thing or two about her very tough sport."

Gracie shivered with nervousness while he spoke.

"You can do this," she whispered. "Just be yourself."

Gracie thought for a second about what it meant to just be herself.

She smiled. She knew just the thing.

Gracie tossed the speech to the floor . . . and then cartwheeled across the stage.

The crowd of students cheered.

As they quietened down,
Gracie climbed onto the stool
next to the microphone. She
glanced at Headmistress Pekoni,
who was frowning at her. But that
didn't bother Gracie. She knew
exactly what to do.

"Hello, Wilbur Academy!" she said. "I am very happy to be back at my old school. I was supposed to give a speech, but I thought we should try something else. Would anyone like to ask me a question?"

A hundred hooves shot up. Gracie curled her tail.

Yes, she could do this.

GLOSSARY

athlete   person who plays sports

champion   someone who is the best at something

demonstrate   show someone how to do something

interview   ask someone questions to find out more about something

lecture   talk to an audience

lecture theatre   room or building with a stage, used for gatherings or shows

passel   large number or amount

volunteer   offer to do something without pay

TALK ABOUT IT!

1. Gracie was nervous about giving her speech. Have you ever been nervous about something? What did you do to calm yourself down?

2. Gracie felt very young when she talked to the headmistress. Have you ever felt that way? What could you do to help convince an adult to listen to you?

3. Gracie tried to teach Coach how to perform some moves. Teaching requires patience. Talk about a time you have had to be patient.

WRITE ABOUT IT!

1. Pretend you are nervous Gracie. Write a letter to yourself to help you to calm down before your big speech.

2. Write a letter to Coach. How could you thank him for trying so hard?

3. Pretend you are Ham Edwards. Write an article for the school paper about Gracie's visit.

About the author

Marsha Qualey is the author of many books for readers young and old. Though she learned to swim when she was very young, she says she has never tried any of the moves and spins Gracie does so well.

Marsha has four grown-up children and two grandchildren. She lives in Wisconsin, USA, with her husband and their two non-swimming cats.

About the illustrator

Kristyna Litten is an award winning children's book illustrator and author. After studying illustration at Edinburgh College of Art, she now lives and works in Yorkshire in the UK, with her pet rabbit Herschel.

Kristyna would not consider herself a very good swimmer as she can only do the breaststroke, but when she was younger, she would do a tumble roll and a handstand in the shallow end of the pool.

THE WONDERFUL, THE AMAZING, THE PIG-TASTIC GRACIE LAROO!

Discover more at www.raintree.co.uk

- Find out more about Gracie and her adventures.

- Follow the Water Sprites as they craft their routines.

- Figure out what you would do . . . if you were the awesome Gracie LaRoo!